All-Star Sports Story
series

TJ'S SECRET
PITCH

FRED BOWEN

PEACHTREE
ATLANTA

Ω

Published by
PEACHTREE PUBLISHERS
1700 Chattahoochee Avenue
Atlanta, Georgia 30318-2112

www.peachtree-online.com

Cover design by Thomas Gonzalez and Maureen Withee
Book design by Melanie McMahon Ives and Loraine M. Joyner

Printed in the United States of America
10 9 8 7 6 5 4 3 2 1
First Revised Edition

Library of Congress Cataloging-in-Publication Data

Bowen, Fred.
    T. J.'s secret pitch / written by Fred Bowen.
        p. cm.
    Summary: In his determination to pitch for his neighborhood baseball team, twelve-year-old T. J. adopts the unorthodox style of the legendary Rip Sewell.
    ISBN 978-1-56145-504-1 / 1-56145-504-0
    [1. Baseball--Fiction. 2. Determination (Personality trait)--Fiction.] I. Title.
II. Title: TJ's secret pitch.
    PZ7.B6724Tj 2009
    [Fic]--dc22
                                        2009017031

For Liam,
my favorite left-hander,
and
for Kerry Margaret,
my favorite right-hander.

ONE

T. J. Burns ran out the front door with his baseball glove and a dream. More than anything else in the world, he wanted to be a baseball pitcher. T. J. looped his baseball glove onto the handlebars of his bicycle and pedaled toward the practice field.

He was in a hurry. Today was the first day of baseball practice.

On his way, T. J. saw one of his teammates from the Pirates. "Hi, Nicole!" called T. J., skidding to a stop in front of her house. "Are you going to practice?"

"Sure," said Nicole as she bumped her bike down her front steps. "You going?"

"Yep. I'm going to ask Mr. Upton if I can pitch this year," T. J. said proudly.

"Gee," Nicole said as she and her bike cleared the last step and came to a stop in front of T. J., "aren't you kinda shrimpy to be a pitcher? I mean, aren't most pitchers, um, you know...bigger...like Matty or Scott?"

T. J. straightened up on his bicycle seat. "I'm not that small. I'm taller than you," he said, a little too loudly.

"No way!" Nicole answered, lowering her bike to the ground. "Come on, back to back, let's measure."

T. J. swung his leg around his bike seat, knocked down the kickstand, pulled himself to his full height, and walked over to Nicole.

The two friends quickly turned away from each other and scooted backward until they bumped. T. J. placed his left hand flat against his head and moved it slowly across his hair. Much to his disappointment his fingertips hit the back of Nicole's head.

"See, I told you so," Nicole said. "I'm two inches taller than you. Easy."

T. J. didn't feel like talking. He got on his

bike, and Nicole got on hers. The two of them pedaled in silence to the practice field.

Eventually, Nicole broke the silence: "At least you get to play second base, T. J. I'd love to play infield."

"I don't want to play second base. I want to be a pitcher," said T. J., who still couldn't believe that Nicole was two inches taller.

Oh, how T. J. wanted to be a pitcher! Earlier that spring, right after the winter snows had melted and long before most kids had started thinking about baseball, T. J. was practicing his windup.

He propped an old mattress against the fence in his backyard and painted a box about the size of a twelve-year-old's strike zone on it. Every day, rain or shine, T. J. would pitch baseballs into the mattress.

Thump. Thump. Thump. The balls would plunk against the mattress. Day after day, T. J. would fire fastballs and dream of standing on the mound.

Some days Bobby Drummer, T. J.'s best friend and the Pirates regular left fielder, would drop by and bring his older brother's catcher's mitt. Bobby would squat down in front of the mattress, give T. J. a target, and call balls and strikes for the would-be Pirates' hurler.

That was a month ago. Now it was the first day of practice. When T. J. and Nicole pulled up to the practice field, they hopped off their bikes and joined the team. T. J. saw Scott, the Pirates tall star pitcher, warming up on the sidelines. Scott's long, loose delivery sent the ball flying in a blur to the dead center of the catcher's mitt. *Thwack!*

Bobby Drummer ran in from left field when he saw T. J. and Nicole. "Hey," he called. "You guys are late! Come on, let's get going."

T. J. and Nicole jogged out toward Bobby and when they caught up with him, Bobby asked, "Are you gonna ask Mr. Upton if you can pitch?"

"Sure," T. J. said confidently as he glanced at Nicole. "I've been practicing all month."

"Well, go ahead and ask him," Nicole dared. "He's standing right over there."

"I think I will," said T. J. He broke away

from Bobby and Nicole and walked over to Mr. Upton.

Mr. Upton was a friendly older man who had coached the Pirates for years. "Hi, T. J.," he said. "How's my second baseman?"

"Fine, Mr. Upton," said T. J., looking up at Mr. Upton and squinting from the sun. "But, um, I was wondering if I could try pitching this year?"

Mr. Upton's smile disappeared. "Gee, T. J.," he said. "I was thinking that Matty or Scott would pitch for us. Scott pitched last year and Matty has the strongest arm in the club. You've got to admit that. And anyway, who would play second base?"

T. J. was ready for that one. "Nicole could play second, Mr. Upton. She played it some last year and did a good job." T. J. pleaded, "Please let me pitch, Mr. Upton. I practiced every day for a month! Just give me a chance."

Mr. Upton's smile returned to his face. "Okay, T. J., why don't you pitch batting practice and show us what you've got?" Turning toward the clump of teammates pulling gloves and balls out of their knapsacks, Mr. Upton said, "C'mon kids! Let's get started. We're going to have some batting practice. Scott, you'll pitch a little later. We're going to give T. J. a chance to show us what he can do."

T. J.'s heart jumped as he ran out to the mound. Bobby trotted by on his way out to his familiar left-field position. "Come on, T. J.!" he called, encouraging his best friend. "Just like we practiced. Smoke it by 'em."

T. J. nodded and toed the rubber just as he had dreamed of doing a thousand times before in his backyard. He looked right into the eye of the batter, Lee Wasserman, one of the the better hitters on the Pirates team. T. J. started his windup and hurled the baseball with all his might.

Whack! Lee smacked the ball over the shortstop's head for a clean single. Bobby hustled his throw back into the infield as Lee teased T. J., "There goes your no-hitter!"

T. J.'s face reddened, then he took a deep breath. He went into his windup and threw the second pitch even harder.

6

Whack!

The ball sailed over the surprised center fielder's head.

"There goes your shutout," Lee laughed.

T. J. shook his head and pushed his fist into his glove. This was trickier than throwing balls against a mattress. T. J. wound up again.

Whack! Another hit. T. J. kept pitching and Lee kept hitting.

Finally, Mr. Upton called for another batter. "Come on, Kevin. Step up to the plate. Swing level and don't try to kill it."

Kevin Vincent, the Pirates stocky star shortstop, stepped to the plate. He cocked his bat behind his batting helmet and glared at the pitcher.

T. J. went into his motion and threw his best heater to the plate.

Whack! The ball sailed toward left field. Bobby Drummer scrambled back to the fence but ran out of room. He watched the ball drop far behind the old green fence.

"Meatballs!" Kevin yelled, grinning ear to ear. "My favorite food. Come on, T. J.—put another one of your meatballs on my dinner plate!"

"That's enough of that, Kevin," scolded Mr. Upton from the sidelines. Then the coach looked at T. J. and said, "Try to keep the ball down in the strike zone."

T. J. followed Mr. Upton's advice on the next pitch, but Kevin slashed a hard grounder past Nicole at second base.

T. J. tried everything. Fastballs inside. Fastballs outside. Fastballs up, down, and all around, but nothing seemed to work. Pirate after Pirate paraded to the plate and pounded T. J.'s pitches. Even Paul "Jellybean" Jones cracked a couple deep into the outfield.

After what seemed forever, Mr. Upton called for another pitcher. T. J. trudged off the mound with his head hung low.

"Not bad, T. J.," said Mr. Upton, trying to be nice. "You have a good windup and you get the ball over the plate. Maybe we can use you in relief this year. But I really think we need you at second base."

T. J. nodded but never looked up. All of

his practicing and dreaming had come to nothing.

Then Mr. Upton turned to the infield and called: "Nicole, why don't you take center? Matty, you come in and pitch. T. J., you take second."

T. J. scuffed off to second, kicking the dirt every step of the way.

"You did okay, T. J.," Nicole said gently. "You'll get a chance to pitch."

"Yeah, sure," T. J. answered. "Maybe we'll get a fifty-run lead in some game, and I'll get to pitch to the last batter."

Nicole started to trot out to center field, then glanced over her shoulder. "Face it, T. J., kids like us never get to be stars."

That night at dinner, T. J. didn't feel like eating. He idly pushed his green beans into the shape of a baseball diamond. He took a spoonful of his mashed potatoes and made a pitcher's mound. Then he sunk a green bean upright into the potatoes and stared at it.

"Stop playing with your food, T. J.," his mom scolded. "Eat your beans."

T. J. scooped the bean off the pitcher's mound.

"How was school today, T. J.?" asked his dad.

"Okay."

"How was practice?"

"All right."

"Do you want some chicken?"

"Nah, I'm not that hungry."

"Are you feeling all right, Teej?" asked Mrs. Burns.

"Sure," said T. J. "Can I please be excused to do my homework?"

"Homework?" T. J.'s mom asked with a shocked voice. "Feel his forehead, Tom, he must be sick."

"Are you okay, T. J.?" asked Mr. Burns.

"I'm fine. I just have a lot of homework," he said.

Mr. and Mrs. Burns looked at each other. Then Mr. Burns looked at T. J., shrugged, and said, "You're excused."

T. J. ran up to his room and closed the door. He grabbed his glove and baseball off his dresser and flopped on his bed. He flipped the ball up toward the ceiling, caught it, and threw it up again and again and again. His rhythm was broken by a knock at the door.

T. J.'s father poked his head in. "Can I come in?"

"Sure, Dad. I was just about to get to my homework," T. J. mumbled.

Mr. Burns sat down on the edge of T. J.'s bed and asked, "Did everything go all right at practice?"

T. J. could not answer. He could feel his throat tighten and tears coming to his eyes.

"Did Mr. Upton let you pitch today?" his father asked.

Now T. J. was crying. He felt a little silly—twelve years old and crying like a baby. He buried his wet cheeks into the warmth of his father's arms. Mr. Burns patted his son's sandy-brown hair and said softly, "It's all right, Teej. Tell me what happened at practice."

T. J. nodded and found his voice between his tears. "It was terrible, Dad. I couldn't get anybody out. Everybody got hits. Even Jellybean hit the fence with one."

T. J.'s father smiled. "Well, think how happy you made Paul feel."

T. J. stopped crying and, without losing his grip on the ball, wiped his eyes with the back of his hand. Then he smiled a weak grin. "You should have seen old Jellybean,

Dad," he said. "He practically danced around the bases."

T. J. smacked the baseball into his glove really hard. "I'll never get a chance to pitch now," he blurted out.

"Teams need second basemen, too," his father reminded him.

"But I practiced so hard!"

"I know you did and I know you feel rotten. But sometimes we can't get what we want no matter how much we want it or how hard we work to get it."

"Yeah, I know. I know."

Then T. J.'s father came up with an idea. "Say, how about coming down to the park and watching my softball game tonight? I think Bobby is going to be there with his dad."

"You mean it?" asked T. J. "Even though it's a school night?"

"I think we can make an exception to that rule. Mom won't mind and you deserve some reward for all your hard work. Besides, it's a special occasion. It's the opening game of our season."

"Great!" exclaimed T. J. as he scrambled off the bed, happy once again. "What position are you playing this year?"

His father looked at the floor and then back at T. J.

"Pitcher," he answered.

THREE

Bobby and T. J. sat in the cool darkness of the grandstands. Out on the field under the bright lights, his dad's team, the Screaming Demons, was warming up. Decked out in their spanking new red-and-white uniforms, the players threw softballs back and forth. T. J.'s dad stood on the mound, practicing his pitches. He rocked back, then glided forward with a bowling motion, lofting the ball underhand in a gentle arc. The fat white ball seemed to hang in the air, then started down and settled into the catcher's glove.

"Man, Dad isn't going to get anybody out if he keeps throwing meatballs like that," T. J. said.

"Yeah, the ball looks like a big, white balloon heading to the plate. I wouldn't mind grabbing a bat and taking a few cuts myself," laughed Bobby.

The leadoff batter for the Diamond Jokers stepped to the plate.

Mr. Burns rocked back and gently floated the first pitch to the plate. "Strike!" the umpire called. The batter hadn't even swung at the pitch.

Mr. Burns lobbed the next pitch a little higher.

Crack! The batter lifted a harmless fly ball out to left field. The Screaming Demons left fielder settled under it for the first out.

The next batter smacked a one-hopper to the shortstop, which the shortstop fielded easily and gunned over to first. The third batter, a real power hitter, hit a long fly ball out to center field. Bobby's dad, Dan Drummer, raced back and made a terrific over-the-shoulder catch deep in center field.

T. J. and Bobby exchanged high fives in

the stands as the Screaming Demons trotted off the field.

"A one-two-three inning!" T. J. said in amazement. "Your dad made a great catch, Bobby!"

"Where do you think I learned to play outfield?" said Bobby. "Your dad did great too. He's got a no-hitter going."

"He won't throw a no-hitter lobbing the ball to the plate," T. J. pointed out.

"I don't know," Bobby answered. "He must be doing something right. He's getting people out."

Mr. Burns did not throw a no-hitter, but the Screaming Demons won 7–3 in a hard-fought game. T. J.'s dad helped with a single up the middle that drove in two runs. But most of all, Tom Burns pitched. He threw great, high meatballs that no one seemed to be able to hit.

After the game, T. J. and his dad got into the car and started home.

"How did you like the game?" Mr. Burns asked as he playfully rubbed the top of T. J.'s head.

"Great, Dad!" said T. J. "You did a super job pitching. How did you get so many people out just lobbing the ball?"

Mr. Burns laughed. "Heck, I didn't get anybody out. My fielders got them out. That's what they are there for."

"You must have done something right, Dad—the Diamond Jokers only scored three runs!"

"Well, first, I didn't walk anybody. There's no defense for a base on balls. Second, I stayed ahead of the hitters. The batter will swing at a pitch a little outside the strike zone if you have a couple of strikes on him. And finally, I moved the ball around in the strike zone. Put it a little high, a little low, inside, outside, and changed speeds a bit. That keeps the hitter off balance. You know what Warren Spahn said about hitting and pitching, don't you?"

"I don't even know who Warren Spahn is," T. J. answered.

"He was a pitcher back around the 1940s and 50s. One of the best. Won 363 games," Mr. Burns said. "Anyway, he said, 'Hitting is timing. Pitching is upsetting timing.' You know, breaking the hitter's concentration."

"Yeah," said T. J.

T. J.'s dad smiled and pulled into the Burnses' driveway. He opened his door and said, "Come on, T. J., let's get you to bed. It's a school day tomorrow."

T. J. sat in the dark for a moment and wondered. Maybe, just maybe, there *was* a way for him to become a pitcher.

FOUR

The next afternoon in school, T. J. glanced at the clock for the twenty-hundredth time: 2:38. Just two minutes to go.

"Remember your permission slips for next week's class trip," Ms. Maggio reminded the class. "And check over your homework essays carefully. I want your best work."

The bell finally rang. T. J. slung his backpack over his shoulder and bolted for the door.

"Not so fast, T. J.," cautioned Ms. Maggio. "Bus kids first."

T. J. waited anxiously at his desk.

"You want to throw the ball around this

afternoon, T. J.?" Nicole asked. "We don't have practice."

"Yeah, sure, come over later," T. J. said as the last of the bus kids walked out the door.

"Walkers and bikers may go," announced Ms. Maggio.

"See ya later," yelled T. J. He flew out the door, hopped on his bike, and pedaled furiously toward home. He turned into the driveway, took his hands off the handlebars, and reached above his head. His hands grabbed hold of the low branch of a sturdy maple tree beside his house. T. J.'s bike, now riderless, veered off to the side and fell in a clattering heap. T. J. swung for a moment from the branch and then dropped to the ground.

He went straight to the garage and dragged out his old pitching mattress. After setting the mattress against the back fence, he ran inside the house and grabbed his glove, some baseballs, and a wastebasket. T. J. placed the basket just below the strike zone he had drawn on the mattress.

Still in his school clothes, T. J. paced off

46 feet from the mattress and the basket. He went into his familiar windup. Only this time, he did not fire the ball at the strike zone. Instead, he slowed his arm down and lobbed the ball overhand. The ball plunked high against the mattress and plopped into the basket.

Ball one. Too high. T. J. would have to get the ball down. His second pitch was a little lower, but still too high.

Finally, with his third pitch, the ball floated through the air, hit just below the blue box on the mattress, and settled into the wastebasket for a perfect strike.

For more than an hour, T. J. lobbed the ball against the mattress. Back and forth he walked, collecting the baseballs from in and around the wastebasket. With each pitch, T. J. gained control and confidence.

"Hey, aren't you out of your school stuff yet?" Nicole asked as she rounded the corner to T. J.'s backyard. "I thought you wanted to throw the ball around. I even got Bobby to come over."

"What's with the dinky trash can, T. J.?"

Bobby asked, eyeing the mattress and the wastebasket.

"Nothing," said T. J., smiling with embarrassment. "I was just working on something." He tried to keep a straight face, but he couldn't keep from grinning.

"Come on, T. J., what's going on?" Nicole asked. She was confused, and T. J. could tell she wanted a straight answer.

"Okay, okay. I'm practicing a new pitch."

"What?" asked Bobby. "It better not be a curve. Mr. Upton won't let us throw curves—says it will hurt our arms."

"Don't worry, it's not a curve," said T. J.

"Is it a knuckle ball?" asked Nicole.

"Nope."

"Well, what is it? Show us!" demanded Nicole, getting more impatient by the minute.

T. J. went into his windup and tossed his overhead lob to the mattress.

"You gotta be kidding!" Bobby blurted out. "That's kindergarten stuff."

"My dad did all right with it last night," T. J. retorted.

"That's different!"

"How come?"

"That's *softball!*"

"So what? A baseball is smaller, so it will be even harder to hit."

"Why don't you guys stop arguing," Nicole interrupted, "so we can go down to the field and try it out?"

"Fine with me," said Bobby. "Let's go."

The three friends collected a couple of baseballs and a bat, hopped on their bicycles, and headed for a nearby park.

T. J. walked out to the mound while Bobby practiced his swing at the plate.

"Why don't you play left field, Nicole?" Bobby asked, pointing the bat to the outfield. "And way, way back. I'm gonna slug these softball pitches."

Nicole hustled out to left. T. J. took a deep breath and went into his windup. The ball sailed slowly toward the plate. Bobby stepped forward and swung with all his might, but the bat hit only air. The ball bounced behind home plate and rolled to the backstop.

Bobby stared at T. J. in disbelief. "Give me another one," he growled.

T. J. concentrated really hard and threw another pitch, higher and softer than the one before. Again, Bobby swung too hard and missed. The next pitch Bobby managed to tap lightly, and T. J. caught it easily.

"That's one out," T. J. said.

"I'm still *way, way* out here," teased Nicole.

"Stay there," yelled Bobby. "I'll hit you one. No problem."

But he didn't. T. J. kept moving the ball around, changing the arc and speed, and Bobby kept missing or tapping easy grounders to the left side of the infield.

Finally Nicole announced, "It's my turn." She jogged toward home plate.

"Fine," Bobby said, throwing the bat into the dirt.

Nicole stepped in at the plate. The Pirate outfielder did better than her teammate but still had trouble timing T. J.'s soft tosses. She hit a few on the fat part of the bat, but she could not knock the lobs very far.

Finally, the three friends called it quits and sat in the shaded dirt behind home plate with their backs resting against the backstop.

"That pitch is a lot tougher to hit than I thought," Nicole said.

Bobby had to agree. "Yeah. I thought I would murder the ball."

"You guys swung at some bad pitches," T. J. said. "I've got to practice getting the ball over."

"Well, the ball was going so slow, I wanted to swing at everything," said Bobby.

Nicole nodded. "And when we did hit it, it didn't go anywhere because the ball was going so slow."

T. J. laughed. So did Bobby and Nicole, but not as hard as T. J. Then T. J. got serious. "Okay, I can get you guys out, but do you think the pitch can work on anybody else?"

"I don't know. Conor Kilgore might hit one or two clear out of town," Nicole said, referring to the Cardinals' star slugger. "But it might work with a lot of other kids."

"It doesn't matter anyway, T. J.," said Bobby. "Matty and Scott are going to do all the pitching this year. Mr. Upton's not going to let you pitch."

"Maybe not, but we play two games a week, and maybe some of them will get rained out. When we make them up, we'll end up playing three games in one week," said T. J., who had already given this possibility a lot of thought. "Mr. Upton's going to need a third pitcher then."

"Or, like you said yesterday, T. J.," Nicole said with a smile, "maybe we'll get so far ahead that Mr. Upton will let you pitch an inning or two."

"So all we have to do," Bobby said, "is to score about twenty runs some game so T. J. will get his chance."

"Either that," T. J. said, grinning, "or pray for rain."

FIVE

The baseball season came, and the chill of April gave way to the warming promise of summer.

Every day T. J. ran out to the backyard to practice his secret pitch. He lobbed thousands of baseballs against the mattress. Some he threw high and slow like short pop flies. Others he threw a little lower and harder. Still others he would throw low and ever so slow as if the ball were moving through molasses.

The Pirates were doing just fine without T. J. pitching. They battled the Cardinals for first place throughout the season.

T. J. was having a good year at second base. He got his share of hits and committed hardly any errors.

Still, T. J. was not quite happy. He was hoping against hope that he would get a chance to pitch. But his chance had not come. Even the weather was against him. The spring remained dry, and T. J. remained at second base.

One evening late in the season, T. J. arrived at the baseball field in his Pirates uniform: black hat with a gold *P*, black shirt, and white baseball pants. T. J. was early, and hardly anyone else was there.

T. J. spied Joe Small, a teenager who was the official scorekeeper of the games. Joe was sitting in one of the dugouts, scribbling in a notebook.

"Hey, Joe, how'd the Cardinals do last night?" T. J. asked, taking a seat on the bench.

"Beat the Braves 5–2. Conor hit another homer last night. That makes six."

"What are the standings? Are we still in first place?"

Joe took a page from his notebook and handed it to T. J. "I just figured them out yesterday, before last night's game." T. J. looked at the neatly typewritten standings.

LEAGUE STANDINGS

TEAM	W	L
Pirates	12	2
Cardinals	11	2
Yankees	8	6
Red Sox	7	7
Braves	4	9
Dodgers	4	10
White Sox	2	12

"If you add last night's win, you and the Cardinals are tied," Joe observed. "Looks like the town championship will come down to the last game of the year between you and the Cardinals."

T. J. handed the paper back to Joe and wandered out to the mound. He stood at the hard rubber slab in the middle of the packed, dark brown clay and thought, *Four more games. I wonder if I'll ever get a chance to pitch from this mound.*

Then T. J. went into his windup and threw an imaginary baseball toward home plate, 46 feet away.

Just then, Bobby and Nicole arrived, interrupting T. J.'s daydream.

"Hey, T. J., you pitching tonight?" they teased.

T. J. smiled, shook his head, and joined his friends.

"Are we gonna win tonight?" he shouted in a pregame psych up.

"Sure," Bobby said. "I'm wearing my lucky socks. We've won seven games in a row and I've worn these same socks each game. I'm telling ya, they are lu-ckee!"

"You make your parents wash the same socks for every game?" Nicole asked in disbelief.

"Wash 'em?" Bobby said in horror. "That would ruin their luck. I'm not washing these socks until we lose or the season ends."

"Oh, gross!" Nicole gasped. "They must really stink!"

Bobby shrugged. "So what if they do? I'm way out in left field most of the game."

"I'm glad I'm in right field," Nicole said as she looked over at T. J. and rolled her eyes.

T. J. laughed.

But later, T. J. started thinking that Bobby's socks might just be lucky, because that evening the Pirates played their best game of the season.

In the first inning with two out, the Pirates loaded the bases. Nicole slashed a hard hit down the right field line and raced to second base as two runs scored. The Pirate bench exploded in cheers.

"Way to go, Nicole!"

"Big hit!"

T. J. followed with a hard liner to center field, and the Pirates led 4–0 after one inning.

With one out in the second, the White Sox got their first hit, a liner to the left, which Bobby got back to second in no time. The next White Sox batter smacked a hot grounder to T. J.'s right. T. J. took two quick steps and made a backhand stab with his outstretched mitt. He then flipped the ball to Kevin Vincent covering second base, who touched the bag and threw to first.

Double play!

Again the Pirate bench was full of back slaps and high fives.

By the end of the fourth inning, the Pirates led 12–0. As they took the field in the top of the fifth, some of the Pirates crowded around Mr. Upton and begged to play different positions.

"Can I catch next inning?" Kevin asked.

"Can I play infield, Mr. Upton?"

"Can I play center?"

Sitting on the bench, Bobby nudged T. J., who was bending forward and reaching under the bench for his glove. "Now's your chance, T. J. Why don't you ask Mr. Upton if you can pitch?"

T. J. was up in a flash. "Can I pitch, Mr. Upton?" T. J. asked.

Mr. Upton looked at the players crowded around him and waved them out into the field. "Let's go. No substitutions this inning. Get out on the field."

From second base, T. J. watched Mr. Upton talking to Joe Small near the Pirates on-deck circle. Mr. Upton was pointing at the scorebook, and Joe was nodding as he wrote in the book.

Scott breezed through a one-two-three inning, including two strikeouts.

When the Pirates hustled off the field at the end of the inning, Mr. Upton met them at the edge of the dugout.

"Listen up," he said, holding up his hand for silence. "We're going to make some changes for the last inning."

Suddenly, the Pirates were quiet.

"Okay. Paul Jones is going to hit for Lee and play third. Kevin moves to catcher. Alan plays shortstop. Michelle, hit for Bobby and play left. Jonathan, you play right field. Nicole moves to second, and T. J. takes Scott's place on the mound."

SIX

T. J. squeezed onto the bench between Bobby and Nicole and began to pound his glove nervously.

"All right, T. J.," Bobby said, jostling his buddy, "on the mound!" Bobby cupped his hands over his mouth, deepened his voice to sound like a ballpark announcer, and said solemnly, "Your attention please, now pitching for the Pirates, number 12, Thomas John 'T. J.' Burns."

Nicole rocked back with laughter. T. J. stared ahead and kept pounding his glove.

"Hey, T. J.," shouted Kevin Vincent from the end of the bench, "let's get a few pitches by them, okay? I want to do some catching. I don't want to just watch them hit it."

"Don't worry," Bobby called back. "They won't even touch it."

Bobby turned to T. J. "I bet nobody comes within a foot of your pitch."

"Just remember to move it around," Nicole reminded T. J. "And keep it low, those are tough ones to hit. And throw strikes, don't get behind the hitter."

"Okay, okay," T. J. said. "You take care of second base, I'll take care of the pitching."

T. J. stared out at the field and continued pounding his glove. The Pirates put two on the board as Paul "Jellybean" Jones blooped a hit into right field for a two-run single. The Pirates might have gotten even more runs but Kevin Vincent's long fly ball was caught at the wall to end the inning.

Mr. Upton encouraged his team as they took the field. "Okay, Pirates. Last inning. Good defense. Paul, play close to the line. Throw strikes, T. J. Just let them hit it. No walks, we have a 14-run lead. Bobby, warm up T. J. I have to help Kevin with the catcher's equipment."

T. J. trotted out to the mound, then

turned to face home plate. Behind the plate, Bobby squatted in a catcher's stance.

"Come on, T. J.!" Bobby shouted. "Throw strikes, baby. Put it over!"

T. J. lofted his practice pitches in a high arc toward the plate. He moved each pitch up and down within the strike zone, changing the speed and loft of each pitch.

Finally, Kevin Vincent ran out to the plate. Bobby handed him the catcher's mitt as Kevin shouted, "One more, T. J. Coming down."

T. J. floated his last practice pitch to the plate, and Kevin pegged a hard strike to second base. T. J. got the ball after the Pirates tossed it smartly around the horn.

"Play ball!" the umpire shouted, motioning for T. J. to pitch.

T. J. went into his windup and floated his first pitch, like a short pop fly to the plate. The White Sox batter never took his bat off his shoulders.

"Strike one!" the umpire's right hand shot up into the air.

The batter stared open-mouthed at T. J.

and then looked over to the White Sox bench. T. J. smiled slightly as Kevin fired the ball back.

T. J.'s second pitch came in a little lower but just as slow. The batter swung from the heels, missed the ball by a foot and fell to one knee in the batter's box.

"Strike two," the umpire called as the Pirates infield broke into laughter.

"Time," Mr. Upton shouted as he charged out of the Pirates dugout and walked briskly to the mound. "What are you doing, T. J.?" Mr. Upton asked.

"Pitching," T. J. answered, toeing the loose clay dirt on the mound.

"Listen," Mr. Upton said sternly. "I don't want the other team thinking that we are making fun of them or that we are being bad sports."

"But...," T. J. started.

"No buts, T. J. We've got a 14-run lead but that is no reason to fool around with the pitching. Throw strikes, like you did on the first day of practice," said Mr. Upton.

Mr. Upton patted T. J. on the back and

headed back to the dugout. T. J. turned his attention once again to the White Sox batter. He went into his windup and fired a fast ball two feet too high.

"Ball one."

T. J. let up a bit on the next pitch.

Crack! The batter sliced a single past Nicole's outstretched glove.

The next batter smacked the first pitch between the left and center fielders, and the runner on first scampered to third.

T. J. pounded his glove and looked around the bases. Runners on second and third, no outs.

T. J. wound up and fired the next pitch so hard his baseball cap fell off.

Smack! T. J.'s head snapped back to watch the Pirates center fielder, Tyrone Davis, sprinting to the fence. Tyrone leaned back, stuck up his glove and snagged the line shot in his glove just a few feet in front of the fence.

The runners on second and third tagged up as Tyrone hurried the ball back into the infield.

The Pirates led 14-1.

"Don't worry, T. J.," Mr. Upton called from the bench. "Just put it over. Still got a big lead."

The Pirates' lead shrank as three runs crossed the plate on a single, a double, a sacrifice fly, and another single. The inning finally ended when Paul "Jellybean" Jones snared a line shot down the third baseline.

The Pirates had held on to the win, 14–4.

After the teams shook hands, T. J. plopped down onto the Pirate bench. Nicole sat down beside him. "We're still in first, T. J." Nicole smiled. "Hey, why didn't Mr. Upton let you throw your pitch?"

"He thought I was making fun of the other team."

"Well, at least you know the pitch works," Nicole said, gathering up her glove to go.

"What do you mean?"

"That kid for the White Sox missed it by a mile."

SEVEN

After the White Sox game, T. J. did not practice his pitch for several days. The Pirates won another game to keep pace with the Cardinals. But T. J. stayed at second base and felt that somehow his dreams of pitching in a real game had disappeared.

Finally, one warm evening, T. J. gathered his last bit of hope and dragged out the tattered mattress from the garage. He set it up against the fence, trudged 46 feet, and started throwing baseballs again.

A few minutes later, he heard a familiar voice call out, "Hey, what do we have here, a young Rip Sewell?"

T. J. turned and saw his grandfather smiling from his wheelchair.

"Hi, Grandpa. I was just fooling around," T. J. answered.

"Looks like the old eephus pitch to me," said Grandpa.

T. J. scrunched up his face and asked, "What's an eephus pitch?"

"That was Rip Sewell's big pitch back in the 1940s. He used to lob it way up there and everybody would try to kill it," said Grandpa Burns. "Did really well for a while, until Ted Williams got a hold of one back in the 1946 All-Star Game. Knocked it clear out of the park."

The older man moved his wheelchair closer. Grandpa Burns was a big baseball fan. T. J. guessed that his grandpa knew just about everything there was to know about baseball.

"Did you ever see Rip Sewell pitch?" T. J. asked.

"Sure. A couple of times back in the old Polo Grounds," Grandpa said with a big grin. "That was quite a ballpark. Short left and right fields, but almost 450 feet to center field. Sewell had the Giants hitting fly balls out to center all day."

"Why did he throw the eephus pitch, Grandpa?"

"Well," Grandpa said, stroking his chin and trying to remember, "I think he hurt his foot in a hunting accident, and he couldn't get enough of a push from his legs to throw hard. So he came up with the eephus pitch."

"Was he any good?"

"Good?" Grandpa started. "Sure he was good." Then Grandpa Burns motioned to the house with his hands and said, "Why don't you run inside and get your dad's copy of THE BASEBALL ENCYCLOPEDIA and we'll look him up."

T. J. dashed back into the house and returned with a heavy hard-covered book. He handed it to his grandfather, who leafed through the pages as T. J. leaned on the arm of the wheelchair.

"Well, let's see. Settlemire. Severinsen. Seward. Sewell. Truett Banks Sewell. Here we go."

T. J. moved closer to his grandfather and looked over his shoulder to the columns of numbers set below Rip Sewell's name.

Truett Banks ("Rip") Sewell

Bats right, throws right, 6' 1", 180 pounds
Born: May 11, 1907, Decatur, Alabama. Died: Sept. 3, 1989, Plant City, Florida.

Year	Team	W	L	ERA	G	IP	H	BB	SO
1932	Detroit	0	0	12.66	5	10.2	19	8	2
1938	Pittsburgh	0	1	4.23	17	38.1	41	21	17
1939	Pittsburgh	10	9	4.08	52	176.1	177	73	69
1940	Pittsburgh	16	5	2.80	33	189.2	169	67	60
1941	Pittsburgh	14	17	3.72	39	249	225	84	76
1942	Pittsburgh	17	15	3.41	40	248	259	72	69
1943	Pittsburgh	21	9	2.54	35	265.1	267	75	65
1944	Pittsburgh	21	12	3.18	38	286	263	99	87
1945	Pittsburgh	11	9	4.07	33	188	212	91	60
1946	Pittsburgh	8	12	3.68	25	149.1	140	53	33
1947	Pittsburgh	6	4	3.57	24	121	121	36	36
1948	Pittsburgh	13	3	3.48	21	121.2	126	37	36
1949	Pittsburgh	6	1	3.91	28	76	82	32	26
13 years		143	97	3.48	390	2119.1	2101	748	636

W=wins; L=losses; ERA=earned run average; G=games; IP=innings pitched; H=hits;
BB=base on balls (walks); SO=strikeouts

"See, he started in 1932," said Grandpa Burns. "Then I think he got hurt and came back with the eephus pitch. Won twenty-one games in 1943 and 1944."

"Has anyone tried the eephus pitch since then?" T. J. asked.

"Sure they have. No one threw it as often as Sewell, but a couple of pitchers threw it every once in a while. Kept the batter guessing."

"Who threw it, Grandpa?"

"Bill Lee of the Red Sox threw it. They used to call him 'The Spaceman.' Threw it one too many times though. Lobbed one up to Tony Perez of the Cincinnati Reds in the seventh game of the 1975 World Series, and Perez knocked it out of sight. Sox lost 4–3. Nearly broke my heart." Grandpa shook his head at the memory. "Steve Hamilton and Dave LaRoche of the Yankees threw it too. Hamilton called it the 'Folly Floater' and LaRoche called it 'La Lob.'"

"What does eephus mean?" T. J. asked.

"Who knows? That's just what Sewell called it."

Grandpa pointed at the mattress. "Let's see you try it, T. J. Show your old grandpa what you've got."

T. J. walked back to the worn patch of backyard that was his pitcher's mound, wound up, and floated the ball into the air. The ball landed just below the box on the mattress and plopped into the basket. A perfect strike.

"Not bad, T. J.," Grandpa said with a wink of his eye. "Keep practicing. You'll be a pitcher yet." Grandpa swung his wheelchair around and rolled across the patio. With a wave of his hand, the old man turned the corner toward home, just a few blocks away. "See you later, Rip," he called.

T. J. turned, wound up again, and threw another perfect strike. "Rip Sewell," T. J. said softly to himself.

EIGHT

A few days later, T. J. pedaled his bike furiously down to the practice field and skidded to a stop along the outfield fence. Most of the Pirates were already there.

"Hey, T. J.," Bobby called from the field as he tossed a baseball back and forth with Lee Wasserman.

"Hey, guys," T. J. called back. "How did the Cardinals do last night?"

"Didn't you hear? They clobbered the White Sox 14–1," Lee answered. "Conor hit another homer! I think that's seven for the year."

"Eight," Bobby corrected him.

"So both teams are 15–2," T. J. said.

"Yeah," Bobby smiled. "Big game tomorrow. For the town championship. I got my lucky socks ready!"

"You mean your yucky socks," Nicole said, sneaking up in back of Bobby and holding her nose.

Everyone laughed, but then they got serious again.

"Matty is gonna have to pitch a good game tomorrow," Lee said finally.

"Where is Matty?" Nicole asked.

"I don't know," said Bobby. "Mr. Upton's late too."

The Pirates went back to tossing baseballs back and forth under the hot afternoon sun, waiting for Mr. Upton to arrive. Soon Mr. Upton's old station wagon pulled up to the practice field. The coach got out slowly. One look at Mr. Upton's face and T. J. knew that something was wrong.

"Let's have everybody over here on the double," Mr. Upton called out. The boys and girls gathered around quickly.

"I have some bad news, kids," said Mr. Upton. "Matty was hurt in a car accident last night and he won't be able to pitch in tomorrow's game."

The team shouted out questions. Mr. Upton held up his hands for quiet.

"He's okay, just a few bruises," he said. "But he took a really hard bump on the head. The doctors want him to stay in the hospital over the weekend to make sure he is okay. He'll be good as new in a week, but this means we need a pitcher for tomorrow's game. Any volunteers?"

The Pirates looked around at one another. No one seemed anxious to pitch in the biggest game of the year. No one, that is, except T. J. He practically jumped out of his skin as he pushed his hand high in the air and called out, "Me, Mr. Upton! Can I pitch?"

The other kids groaned. "T. J. can't pitch," mumbled Kevin Vincent. "He can't get anybody out." The Pirates nodded in agreement.

"I can too!" T. J. shouted at Kevin.

"Well, let's give him another chance," said Mr. Upton. "I'll call balls and strikes from in back of the pitcher's mound. T. J. will pitch. Nicole will play second. The starting lineup will bat in their usual order. Okay, take the field."

T. J. walked out to the mound and started warming up by lobbing the ball to the catcher. After a few pitches, Mr. Upton stood behind the mound ready to call balls and strikes.

"Do you need any warm-up pitches?" Mr. Upton asked.

T. J. almost laughed. Mr. Upton did not know that T. J. was throwing warm-up pitches.

"No, Mr. Upton, I'm ready."

The first batter was Kevin Vincent. The Pirate shortstop was rubbing his bat, ready to hit. T. J. wound up and threw a high slow one. Kevin cocked his bat and stepped forward, ready to kill the ball.

But he could only stare wide-eyed as the ball floated past.

"Strike one," said Mr. Upton.

"Hey, what are you doing?" Kevin yelled. "Throw a real pitch."

The second pitch was just as high and just as slow. Kevin was ready this time. He swung with all his might and missed the ball by a foot.

"Strike two."

By now, the Pirates were laughing and Kevin's face had turned an angry red. T. J.'s third pitch was a little lower but every bit as slow. Kevin swung so hard that he nearly fell out of his shoes.

"Strike three."

The fielders cheered, and Mr. Upton could not help laughing. "Okay, T. J.," he said gently. "Fun is over. Let's see you really pitch."

"This *is* how I really pitch, Mr. Upton," T. J. said, looking at the ground and feeling a bit embarrassed.

"Where did you get the idea to pitch like that?" asked Mr. Upton.

"My grandpa said Rip Sewell used to pitch like this," said T. J. in an excited voice. "He called it the eephus pitch."

"The eephus pitch?" said Mr. Upton. He had a smile on his face.

"Well, I wasn't getting anybody out throwing the ball fast, so I figured I would try throwing it slow," T. J. said.

"Can you get it over?" Mr. Upton asked.

"Sure, I've been practicing all season."

"He has, Mr. Upton," said Nicole, walking in from her position at second base. "Bobby and I have been practicing with him and we can't hit it. It's really tough."

Mr. Upton stood at the mound looking at Nicole and then back to T. J. "Okay," he said finally, "if you can get the ball over the plate and get people out, then do it. I don't care how you do it just so long as you do it. Next batter."

Lee Wasserman stepped to the plate, but his luck was no better than Kevin's. Finally, he lofted a short fly to left, but Bobby caught it easily.

T. J. pitched to all the Pirate starters and to some of the reserves. T. J. mixed up his pitches and kept the batters guessing. He did not walk anyone and gave up only one hit. Most of the Pirates swung too hard and ended up hitting harmless ground balls or pop flies. Only Bobby and Nicole hit the ball hard at all.

Finally Mr. Upton called out, "Okay, T. J., let's try another pitcher here. You're upsetting the hitters' timing."

T. J. flipped the ball to his coach and trotted out to second base. Mr. Upton tried out a couple more pitchers, but none of the kids did as well as T. J. After practice was over, Mr. Upton called the players together.

"That was a good practice, kids. I think we are going to beat those Cardinals." He paused and looked right at T. J.

"We will go with the same starting lineup," he said. "But Nicole will start at second and T. J. will pitch."

This time, all the Pirates, even Kevin Vincent, cheered.

NINE

T. J. woke with the sun on the day of the big game. He tossed and turned in his bed, trying to get comfortable and trying not to think about the game.

Eventually, T. J. gave up on the idea of sleep. He slipped into a T-shirt and jeans and tiptoed out to the backyard. The wet grass felt cool on his bare feet. He dragged out the mattress and the wastebasket, took his familiar position, and started lobbing baseballs once again.

"Hey, champ. What are you doing up so early?" Tom Burns stood in his bathrobe at the back door with sleep in his eyes and a cup of coffee in his hand.

"Nothing, Dad, just trying to get in some practice."

Tom Burns took a long gulp of coffee and placed the cup on a patio table. "Let me get my glove," he said. T. J.'s dad emerged a few seconds later, slapping the pocket of his well-worn leather mitt.

"Come on, T. J., let's see what you've got," he said, knocking away the wastebasket and crouching in front of the mattress. T. J. lifted his first pitch to the plate.

"Get it down, T. J.," Tom Burns said as he fired the ball back to his son. "You've gotta keep it low in the strike zone."

T. J. and his dad tossed the baseball back and forth. T. J.'s dad shouted out bits of encouragement and advice:

Nice pitch, T. J., nice pitch.

Keep it low. Around the knees.

That's it!

If you pitch it high, keep it above the shoulders.

Put a little spin on it.

Great!

Don't put it waist high. Anybody can hit that one.

After a while, T. J.'s dad held up his hand.

"That's enough, T. J. Let's get some breakfast. You don't want to waste all your best pitches in warm-ups."

The two headed across the patio to the Burnses' back door. Tom Burns rubbed his son's pitching shoulder and said, "How are you feeling, Teej?"

"Kinda nervous, Dad."

"Why is that?"

"I'm not so sure this eephus pitch thing is going to work against the Cardinals," T. J. answered, looking down at the patio.

"Just do your best, T. J. That's all anybody can ask. And anyway, Ted Williams was about the only guy ever to hit a home run off Rip Sewell's eephus pitch. I don't think the Cardinals have Ted Williams, do they?"

"No," T. J. said seriously as he looked into his father's face. "But they *do* have Conor Kilgore."

TEN

The sun was high and hot when the Pirates and the Cardinals gathered for the game that would decide the town championship.

The Pirates swarmed around Mr. Upton for their final instructions. "Okay, kids. We're up first. Here's the lineup. Lee leads off playing first base. Bobby's in left. Kevin's at short. Marcus is catching and batting cleanup. Alan is at third. T. J., you're up sixth and on the mound. Nicole's at second. Ty is in center. And Michelle is in right. Get some hits for T. J. and give him some good defense. Let's go!"

Mr. Upton's encouragement did nothing for the Pirates in the top of the first. The

Pirates went down one-two-three to Chris Elmer, the Cardinals fireballing ace pitcher.

T. J.'s heart was beating fast as he trotted out to the mound. His first few warm-up pitches were short and in the dirt. But soon T. J. got into his rhythm, and the ball floated over the plate.

The Cardinals were laughing as they watched T. J. warm up. They teased him from the sidelines.

"Come on, T. J., can't you throw any harder than that?"

"Softball's at the girls' field, T. J."

"Why don't you throw underhand?"

The Cardinals were not laughing at the end of the inning. The first two Cardinals struck out, and Conor Kilgore popped out to the infield.

The Pirates were all high-fives as they returned to the bench.

"Thatta way, T. J.," Bobby said, clapping T. J. on the back. "You're doing great."

"Did you see Conor's face when he swung?" Nicole added with a grin. "Man, he looked like he was trying to hit it into next week."

The game settled into a strange pitcher's duel and remained a scoreless tie through three innings. The Pirates could only manage one hit off Chris Elmer's blazing fastball, while the Cardinals swung too hard and popped T. J.'s "meatballs" high into the air. Time after time, the Pirate fielders settled under the soft flies for easy outs.

The Pirates broke the scoreless tie in the top of the fourth. T. J. struck out on three pitches, but Nicole slapped a single into right field. Tyrone Davis laid down a perfect bunt and scampered to first base. Michelle Fortney knocked a slow roller that just stayed fair along the first base line. The Cardinals first baseman gathered up the grounder and stepped on first, but the runners moved up.

With runners on second and third, the Pirates leadoff hitter, Lee Wasserman, came to the plate.

The Pirate bench was up and cheering.

"Come on, Lee, little bingle baby."

"Only takes one!"

"Make it be in there."

"Be a sticker, Lee, be a sticker."

Lee timed a Chris Elmer fastball just right and lined a hard smash into left center field. Two Pirates scampered across home plate. At the end of the inning, the Pirates were ahead 2–0!

The Cardinals started to hit T. J.'s pitches harder in the bottom of the fourth. They timed a couple of high lobs perfectly and rapped a pair of sharp singles.

With two outs and players on first and third, the Cards' top slugger, Conor Kilgore, came to the plate.

T. J.'s first two pitches were in the dirt. Two balls, no strikes. Now he was in real trouble. If he walked Conor, the bases would be loaded.

T. J. threw the next pitch over the heart of the plate. *Crack!* Conor swung hard and hit the ball right on the nose.

Bobby Drummer, the Pirates' left fielder, ran back toward the fence in left center field at top speed. He stretched out and jumped for the ball at the last moment.

Bobby tumbled to the ground and rolled over at the base of the fence. T. J. stood on the mound with his heart in his throat. He could not tell whether Bobby had held on.

All the Pirates leapt into the air when Bobby held the ball up. What a catch! The score was still 2–0!

ELEVEN

The Pirates were all over Bobby as they raced back into their dugout. "What a catch!"

"Give that man a Gold Glove."

"Play of the year!"

Mr. Upton interrupted the celebration by calling out, "Kevin leads off. Marcus on deck. Alan in the hole. Let's get some runs!"

T. J. slid between Bobby and Nicole on the bench. "Great catch, Bobby. You really scared me that inning," he said.

"Nothing to it." Bobby gave them a big smile. "It's the lucky socks, I tell you. They make me run faster and jump higher. They are unbelievable."

"They're just unwashed," Nicole joked.

"I'm going to need all the luck I can get," T. J. said.

"You want my socks?" Bobby asked.

T. J. laughed but quickly turned serious again. "Look, the Cardinals are starting to hit the pitch. I was fooling them at first, but now they're catching on. I don't know if I can hold them."

"You're doing a great job," Nicole reassured him.

T. J. looked at the ground and shook his head. "I'm not doing anything," he mumbled. "I'm just lobbing it up there and letting them hit it."

"They haven't scored yet," Nicole pointed out.

"Don't worry, T. J.," Bobby said. "We'll get you some runs."

Bobby was a better left fielder than predictor. The Pirates could not score any runs in the top of the fifth or sixth innings. The Cardinals went down one-two-three in the bottom of the fifth even though they hit T. J.'s meatballs hard.

So the Pirates were still ahead 2–0 when the Cardinals came up for their "last licks" in the bottom of the sixth. "Just three outs!" Mr. Upton called as the Pirates took the field.

But soon, T. J. was in hot water. The Cardinals leadoff hitter smacked a line drive between the right and center fielders and scooted to second base for a stand-up double. The next batter popped up.

But a sharp single sent the leadoff hitter home. The score was 2–1, and the Pirates were hoping, almost praying, for two more outs. The next batter rapped a sharp grounder to Kevin Vincent who gathered in the grounder and flipped the ball to Nicole covering at second base for the second out. One out to go! T. J. stood on the mound sweating under the hot sun. His heart pounded, and the baseball felt like a lead weight in his hand.

"Just one out," pleaded Nicole from second base. That one out did not come on the next batter. Mark Russo, the Cardinals catcher, lashed a liner off the left field wall. A good throw from Bobby Drummer held the tying runner at third.

Players on second and third. Two outs.

The Pirates leading by one slim run. Conor Kilgore was coming to the plate, and Mr. Upton was walking slowly out to the mound.

"How ya doing, T. J.?" Mr. Upton asked with a small smile.

"Okay," T. J. lied.

"Remember that first base is open. If you walk Conor, you can still get the next batter."

"I sure don't want to pitch with the bases loaded," T. J. said.

"I know," said Mr. Upton. "Just be careful. Don't throw any pitches down the pipe to Conor. Keep it inside or outside and try to make him swing at a bad pitch."

Mr. Upton gave T. J. a pat on the back. "You've pitched a great game, T. J. Just one more out."

T. J. kept the first pitch high and inside just like Mr. Upton had said. Conor smacked the ball deep to left. The Pirates held their breath as the home run ball drifted foul.

Strike one. A very long strike one.

T. J. lofted the next two pitches outside the strike zone hoping that Conor would swing at a bad pitch. No such luck. The Cardinals' star slugger was too smart for that. The count went to two balls and one strike.

T. J. lobbed the next one on the inside corner of the plate. Again, Conor ripped the ball down the left field line. The ball fell a few feet short of the fence just inches outside the foul line.

Foul ball. Two balls, two strikes. The Cardinal baserunners, who had been off at the crack of the bat, trotted back to their bases. Once again, Conor Kilgore picked up his bat, looking out at T. J. with a confident smile.

T. J. looked in at the batter without hope. Players on second and third and the Cardinals' best player at bat.

There was no way for T. J. to get the ball past him. Unless...

Of course! T. J. had been lobbing the ball all day. Why not try another surprise? It was worth a chance.

T. J. went into his familiar windup. He

brought his arms above his head, flipped his right arm down along his side and stepped forward.

Only this time T. J. did not slow down and lob the ball. Instead, he whipped his arm around just as he had done a thousand times in the early spring and fired the ball with all his might.

T. J. felt wonderful as the ball left his hand. For the first time since he had started practicing his secret pitch, T. J. felt like an honest-to-goodness pitcher.

His fastball blazed across the outside corner. Conor was so shocked that he never took the bat off his shoulder.

Strike three! The Pirates were town champs!

T. J.'s teammates rushed onto the field and carried T. J. off on their shoulders. As he bounced high above his happy teammates, he spotted his parents and grandpa still cheering from the sidelines. They waved to T. J. and he waved back, grinning from ear to ear.

TWELVE

Later that night, T. J. lay in the stillness of his bedroom. The light from a full moon came through the window and fell in silvery squares on his desk. In the dim light, T. J. could see his baseball glove lying on the corner of the dresser. Tucked safely within the glove was the game ball. T. J.'s dad knocked on the door and poked his head in.

"Still awake?" Tom Burns asked as he sat on the edge of the bed.

T. J. rose up on one elbow. "Yeah. I guess I'm still thinking about the game."

"So how does it feel to be the championship pitcher?"

"Fine, I guess. But you know, I still don't feel like a real pitcher."

"You held the Cardinals to one run," T. J.'s dad said gently. "I call that real pitching."

"I just tricked them, that's all."

"Isn't that what pitching is all about, tricking the batter?"

T. J. thought for a moment. Maybe his dad was right.

"Anyway," Tom Burns said, tousling T. J.'s hair, "are you going to tell Grandpa that Rip Sewell wasn't a real pitcher?"

"No," T. J. laughed.

"You better not, because I know what he'll say if you do." T. J.'s dad lowered his voice so he sounded just like Grandpa Burns. "Why, Rip Sewell won more than twenty games in 1943 and 1944. I call that real pitching." T. J.'s dad rose to go. "You better get some sleep, T. J. You've had a big day. Good night."

"Good night, Dad."

T. J. rolled over on his back, pulled the covers to his chin, and stared at the ceiling. For the hundredth time he thought about the final strike. He remembered how the ball flew from his fingertips just as it had so many times before in his backyard practice sessions and in his daydreams.

Then T. J. remembered the thrill of being paraded around on top of his teammates' shoulders. He was so happy that he did not even mind when Kevin Vincent joked, "Hey, we're lucky that T. J. pitched today. He's so small that he is a cinch to carry around!"

Everyone laughed, even T. J. As they bounced him high in the air, he didn't mind the teasing. Even now, lying in bed and remembering, T. J. did not feel small.

He felt very big indeed.

THE END

RIP SEWELL
THE REAL STORY

T. J.'s grandfather was right—Rip Sewell was a pretty good pitcher.

Born in 1907, Truett "Rip" Sewell joined the Pittsburgh Pirates in 1938. He didn't win any games the first year, but won forty over the next three seasons.

In those years, Sewell did not throw his famous pitch. He only had an average fastball and curveball, so he depended on pinpoint control to get batters out.

Everything changed on December 7, 1941, the day Japan attacked Pearl Harbor and U.S. soldiers started fighting in World War II. Rip Sewell was on a hunting trip with a friend that day. His friend accidently shot him. At the hospital, doctors removed buckshot from Sewell's stomach and legs but could not remove several pellets from his feet.

The injury prevented Sewell from joining the many other major leaguers who fought in World War II. It also forced Sewell to change the way he pitched because he couldn't lean on his feet the same way he used to. He began to experiment with the blooper pitch which he first threw in a game during the 1943 season. The pitch became known as the "eephus" pitch. One of his teammates named it that because, he said, "eephus doesn't mean anything and neither does the pitch."

The pitch may not have meant much, but National League batters had little success hitting it. Sewell posted 21 wins in 1943 and 1944 and pitched in three All-Star games. Unlike T. J., Sewell only threw the pitch about twenty times a game and never with runners on base. (Major league base runners can run the moment the pitcher starts to throw the ball toward home. Little Leaguers have to wait until the ball crosses the plate.)

Sewell lofted the eephus pitch as high as 25 feet, so the ball would be coming almost straight down when it reached the batter. Once, completely frustrated, Cincinnati Reds shortstop Eddie Miller caught the ball in midair and threw it back at Sewell!

Only the great Ted Williams, who played for the Boston Red Sox, ever hit the eephus pitch for a home run. Before the 1946 All-Star Game, Williams asked Sewell if he would throw his famous pitch to him. Sewell signalled Williams when the time came and served up a blooper; the Red Sox slugger knocked it into the seats for a home run.

Sewell retired from baseball after the 1949 season. Years later, doctors amputated his legs below the knees because of problems related to his old hunting injuries. With the help of artificial legs, Sewell remained active, even playing golf and playing it well—he scored in the eighties. This accomplishment is really not very surprising, since Sewell had learned during his baseball career that there is always more than one way to achieve a goal.

ACKNOWLEDGMENTS

The author would like to acknowledge Scot Mondore at the research department at the Baseball Hall of Fame in Cooperstown, New York. Mr. Mondore was gracious and forthcoming with lots of information on pitcher Rip Sewell, and Rip Sewell is not even in the Hall of Fame.

In addition, the author would like to note that the Rip Sewell statistics in chapter seven did indeed come from THE BASEBALL ENCYCLOPEDIA, which is published by Simon & Schuster, Inc., in New York City.

ABOUT THE AUTHOR

One of Fred Bowen's earliest memories is watching the 1957 World Series with his brothers and father on the family's black-and-white television in Marblehead, Massachusetts. Mr. Bowen was four years old.

When he was six years old, he was a batboy for his older brother Rich's Little League team. At age nine, he played on a team himself, spending a great deal of time keeping the bench warm. By age eleven, he was a Little League All Star.

Over a period of thirteen years, Mr. Bowen coached thirty-one different kids' sports teams in soccer, baseball, softball, and basketball.

Mr. Bowen is the author of a number of sports novels for young readers. He lives in Silver Spring, Maryland with his wife Peggy Jackson. His daughter is a college student and his son is a college baseball coach.

Mr. Bowen writes a sports column for kids in the *Washington Post*.

Visit his website at *www.fredbowen.com*.

Want more?

All-Star Sports Story Series